# 100 Years Old with Baby Teeth

## Illustrated by Claudia Wolf

## Written by Deanna Thompson

*For Eliza*

Deanna Thompson lives in Greensboro, N.C., with her husband,
Taft Wireback, and their children,
Travis, Nathaniel and Eliza Wireback.

Copyright 2006.  Published by Journey Stone Creations, LLC.
All rights reserved. Printed in China by Global PSD.
Little Gems is an imprint of Journey Stone
Creations, LLC. First print run, 2006.

**ISBN# 1-59958-000-4**

Visit our web site for other great titles.
www.jscbooks.com

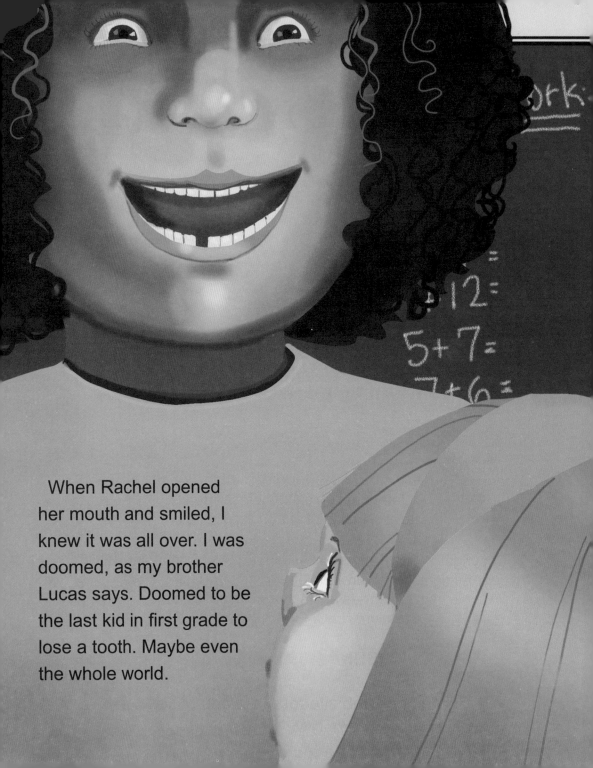

When Rachel opened her mouth and smiled, I knew it was all over. I was doomed, as my brother Lucas says. Doomed to be the last kid in first grade to lose a tooth. Maybe even the whole world.

"It came out last night while I was outside running in circles," Rachel said excitedly, smiling big so a teeny gap in her bottom teeth showed.

"You look stupid when you smile like that," I said.

Rachel stared at me for a second. Then a hurt look came on her face and she turned and ran over to the pavement on the playground, where Mary Elizabeth was jumping rope with Hannah. I felt bad right away. That wasn't nice, I told myself.

But when you're the only kid in your whole class who hasn't lost a tooth yet, you get a little mean sometimes.

"I'll never lose a tooth," I told Mom that night as she dried me off after my bath.

"Yes, of course, you will," said Mom, giving me a quick hug. "Let me look."

She reached in and tried to jiggle one of my bottom front teeth. It didn't move at all. Not one little bit.

"You just have to be patient," she said again. "There's nothing you can do to make your teeth come out before they're ready. They'll get loose when your permanent teeth start pushing on them."

"I'll be 60 years old, and I'll still have all my baby teeth," I protested, making my face into a pout before running off to my room.

The next morning at school, I told Rachel I was sorry.  She said it was okay.

"I want to lose a tooth, too!" I said sadly.

"Maybe Santa Claus will make your tooth fall out if you tell him that's what you want for Christmas," she suggested.

"Great idea!" I said.

That afternoon, when I got home from school, I got out a piece of my brother's notebook paper and a pencil and sat down to write.

Dear Santa,
Forget about that doll I asked for. All I want for Christmas is to lose a tooth. Can you bring me a loose tooth for Christmas?
    Love,
    Caroline

Mom and I put it in an envelope, addressed it to Santa Claus, North Pole, put a stamp on it and then we drove to the post office at Friendly Center and put it in the mailbox.

Christmas came and I found a doll, some books, a basketball and a handy-dandy ice cream maker under the tree. I checked my mouth. No loose teeth.

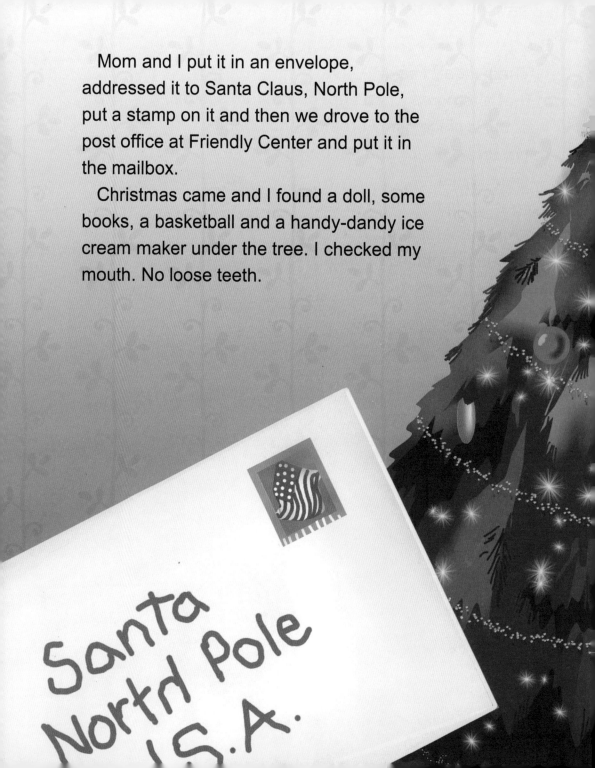

Santa
North Pole
U.S.A.

"I'll never lose a tooth," I told Daddy as we took down the Christmas tree.

"Yes, of course, you will," said Daddy. "All in good time. You just have to be patient. When your tooth is ready to come out, it will."

"I'll be 70 years old, and I'll still have all my baby teeth," I complained.

I waited and waited, and I still didn't have a loose tooth. Then one day, a new girl named Sheila with two beautiful big front teeth came to our class at school.

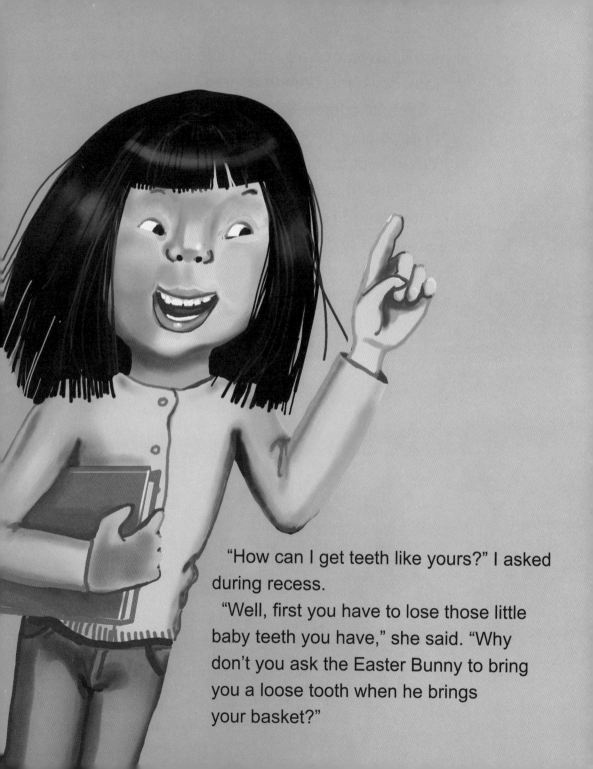

"How can I get teeth like yours?" I asked
during recess.

"Well, first you have to lose those little
baby teeth you have," she said. "Why
don't you ask the Easter Bunny to bring
you a loose tooth when he brings
your basket?"

So that afternoon, I sat down with a piece of pink construction paper and some markers and wrote a letter.

Dear Easter Bunny,

Please don't bring me any candy this Easter. All I want for Easter is to lose a tooth. Can you bring me a loose tooth for Easter?

Love,

Caroline

P.S. One piece of candy would be okay.

Bunny
Bunnyland

"Where do you send mail to the Easter Bunny?" I asked Mom.

Mom and I put my letter in an envelope, addressed it to the Easter Bunny, Bunnyland, put a stamp on it, and then we drove to the post office at Friendly Center and put it in the mailbox.

The Easter Bunny still brought me a basket. It had one piece of candy in it, some books and a yo-yo.

I tried wiggling all of my teeth. Nothing.

"I'll be 80 years old, and I'll still have all my baby teeth," I told Mom as she combed my hair for school.

"Just be patient," she said. "It will come out when it's ready."

I waited and waited. I still didn't have a loose tooth.

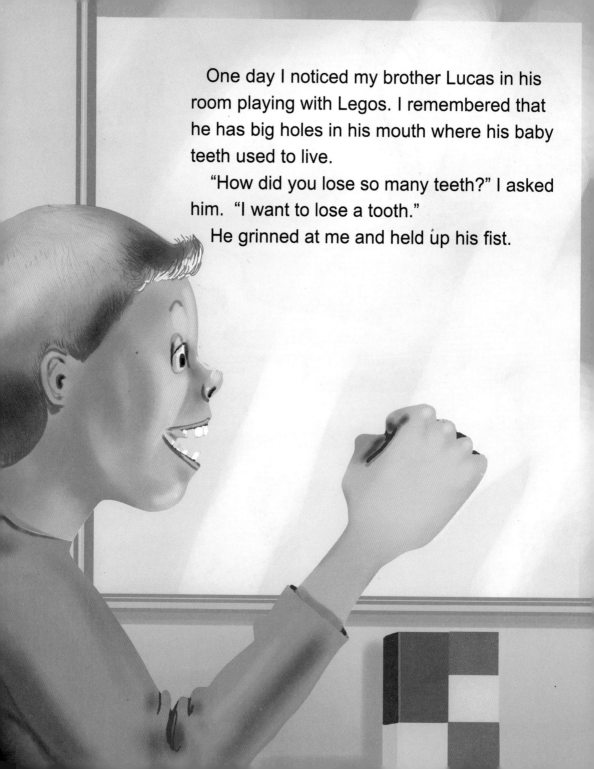

One day I noticed my brother Lucas in his room playing with Legos. I remembered that he has big holes in his mouth where his baby teeth used to live.

"How did you lose so many teeth?" I asked him. "I want to lose a tooth."

He grinned at me and held up his fist.

"How about a nice knuckle sandwich?" he asked. "That will give you a loose tooth!"

I thought about that for a minute, but I didn't think Mom would like it.

"I was just kidding!" Lucas said. "Why don't you ask the Tooth Fairy for a loose tooth? If anybody can bring you a loose tooth, she should be able to do it. She's sure got lots of them."

So I got some lined paper and wrote a letter to the Tooth Fairy.

Dear Tooth Fairy,

I know you mostly get teeth after they fall out. But can you make a tooth fall out, too? If you can, I would like to be first on your list.

Thanks,

Caroline

"Where do you send mail to the Tooth Fairy?" I asked Mom.

Mom and I put my letter in an envelope, addressed it to the Tooth Fairy, Fairyland, put a stamp on it, and then we drove to the post office at Friendly Center and put it in the mailbox.

I waited and waited and waited a really long time. And still no loose tooth.

"I'll be 90 years old, and I'll still have all my baby teeth," I told my mother.

"No, you won't," she said. "Just be patient. Your first tooth will come out when it's ready."

Well, I don't think it's ever going to be ready. That's what I told my next-door neighbor Katie, who's younger than me, and is probably the only other person in the whole wide world who hasn't lost a tooth.

"Why don't you ask God for a loose tooth?" she suggested.

So that night when I said my prayers, I asked God to send me a loose tooth.

Dear God,
I know I usually ask you to bless me and my family and all the people in the whole wide world. And you can still do that tonight. But could you also please help me get a loose tooth?

This time, I addressed my prayer to God, Heaven, and sent it off right then and there through outer space. I didn't even have to drive to Friendly Center to the mailbox! Maybe this will work.

I tried wiggling my teeth the next day. No loose tooth. Days passed and more days passed, and I still didn't have a loose tooth. I was all out of ideas.

"I'll be 100 years old, and I'll still have all my baby teeth," I told my teacher.

"You just have to be patient," Mrs. Hill said.  "There's nothing you can do to make your teeth come out before they're ready. They'll get loose when your permanent teeth start pushing on them."

Then, one day when I was eating lunch at school, I dipped my baby carrot in some ranch dressing and bit down on it and ONE OF MY TEETH MOVED!  It really did.  It was the tooth on the bottom in the middle on the same side as my writing hand. I think that's the right side.

"I have a loose tooth," I yelled, right there at the table. The lunch lady came over to see what was wrong, but when she found out she didn't send me to silent lunch!  Good thing, too, 'cause I couldn't shut up about it.  "I have a loose tooth!" I told everyone I saw.  Mrs. Hill.  Our PE coach.  The special teacher who helps me with my "R" sound.  The bus driver, Mr. Bob.

"I have a loose tooth!" I yelled to Mom as I ran in the house from the bus and threw my backpack in the front hall.

I jiggled it a little that night. The next day and the next day and the day after, I jiggled some more. I turned it one way, then the other, and you know what? On the third day, it came out in my hand, right there in the hallway outside the kitchen.

"See, I told you that your tooth would come out in good time, when it was right for you," Mom said, as I tucked the tooth under my pillow that night.

And so how old was I by then? 100? 90? 80? 70? 60? No, I was 7. And I lost a tooth!